**KLASKY
CSUPO** INC.

Based on the TV series *Nickelodeon Rocket Power*™
created by Klasky Csupo, Inc. as seen on Nickelodeon®

SIMON SPOTLIGHT
An imprint of Simon & Schuster Children's Publishing Division
1230 Avenue of the Americas, New York, New York 10020

Manufactured in the United States of America

First Edition
2 4 6 8 10 9 7 5 3 1

ISBN 0-689-84539-1

JOKE BOOK

by Holly Kowitt

Simon Spotlight/Nickelodeon

New York   London   Toronto   Sydney   Singapore

TABLE OF CONTENTS

HI, TIDE!

Why did the surfer wear a baseball mitt?
HE WANTED TO CATCH A WAVE.

Where does a surfer sleep?
IN A WATER BED.

Why are Reggie and her friends great letter openers?
THEY CAN REALLY RIP!

What does Reggie eat for breakfast?
SHREDDED WHEAT.

How does the ocean say "hi" to the Rockets?
IT WAVES!

Otto: Have you ever seen a man-eating fish?

Twister: Sure, dude.

Otto: Where?

Twister: At the Shore Shack!

When a surfer gets married, what does he say?
I DUDE!

○○○○ ⇨

What kind of hair does a surfer have?

WAVY.

What kind of suit do you wear to a surfer's wedding?

A WET SUIT.

Why did Otto put a TV on his Boogie board?

HE WANTED TO CHANNEL SURF.

8

Why did Reggie put her exam in the ocean?
SHE WANTED TO TEST THE WATERS.

What do sharks order at the Shore Shack?
PEANUT-BUTTER-AND-JELLYFISH SANDWICHES.

9

GNARLY KNOCK-KNOCKS

Knock, knock.

WHO'S THERE?

X.

X WHO?

X-treme sports are awesome, man!

KNOCK, KNOCK.

Who's there?

SEASHORE.

Seashore who?

SEASHORE TEARS IT UP OUT THERE!

knock, knock.

WHO'S THERE?

Crab.

CRAB WHO?

Crab your
board and
let's rip!

KNOCK, KNOCK.

Who's there?

OTTO.

Otto who?

OTTO BE STUDYING—BUT I'M
RIDING WAVES INSTEAD!

○○○○ ⇒

KNOCK, KNOCK.
Who's there?
TECHNO.
Techno who?
TECHNO PRISONERS,
MAN!

Knock, knock.
WHO'S THERE?
Candace.
CANDACE WHO?
Candace go any faster?

HAVE AN ICE DAY!

Why did Twister bring rope
to the hockey game?

HE WANTED TO TIE UP THE SCORE.

What did Otto
say to the
Abominable Snowman?

"CHILL, DUDE!"

○○○○⇨

What animal does Otto refuse to play hockey with?

A CHEETAH.

What's the coolest thing about ice hockey?

THE ICE.

Where do hockey players stay in New York?

The Empire Skate Building.

14

Why does Otto play Monopoly?

HE LIKES BOARD GAMES.

What do hockey players pledge allegiance to?

THE UNITED SKATES OF AMERICA.

o o o o ⇨

Sam: DO YOU EVER GET TIRED OF SNOWBOARDING?

Otto: 'Snow Way!

What do cats play in the winter?
MICE HOCKEY.

POWERGIRLS RULE!

Why does the Rocket gang love snowboarding? 'CAUSE THERE'S NO BUSINESS LIKE SNOW BUSINESS.

Why do fish make lousy hockey players?

THEY DON'T LIKE TO GET CLOSE TO THE NET.

WISH YOU WERE AIR

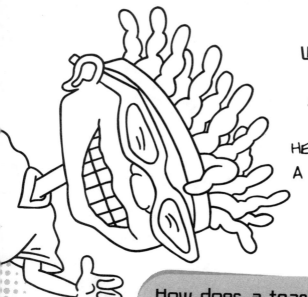

Why did Otto lose the skateboard contest?

HE WAS HAVING A BAD AIR DAY.

How does a teacher go surfing?

ON A BLACKBOARD.

Why is Madtown Skate Park so hot after a tournament?

BECAUSE ALL THE FANS LEAVE.

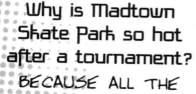

What do you get when a
large rabbit skateboards?

BIG HARE.

What's Otto's favorite
kind of school?

BOARDING SCHOOL.

Why did Otto go to the doctor?
HIS MOVES WERE SICK!

HOW'D YOU DO IN THE SKATEBOARD TOURNAMENT?

Carpenter: I NAILED EVERY MOVE.

Pig: I played dirty.

Janitor: I cleaned up.

Paper towel: I WIPED OUT.

20

Balloon salesman: I BUSTED SOME BIG AIR.

Nurse: I had a sick finish.

Plumber: I only did a half pipe.

Orange: I RAN OUT OF JUICE.

Egg: EVERYONE BEAT ME.

Nail: I got hammered.

JUST SQUIDDING!

Why did Tito put grapes
in his ukulele?

HE WANTED TO HAVE A
JAM SESSION.

Why do hot dogs make good teammates?

'CAUSE EVERYONE'S A WIENER!

What do frogs order
at the Shore Shack?
BURGER AND FLIES.

How do you make
a guava shake?
TAKE IT TO A
SCARY MOVIE!

What animal never
shows off at sports?
THE HUMBLE BEE.

Why did Otto bring soap
to the beach?
THEY WERE PREDICTING SHOWERS.

24

GET WHEEL!

How did Sam learn to skate?

HE TOOK A CRASH COURSE.

What kind of skates
do penguins wear?
POLARBLADES.

Where do pigs go skating
in Ocean Shores?
MADTOWN SKATE PORK.

What do sharks call
in-line skaters?
MEALS ON WHEELS.

26

Which part of florida
has the best skating?
THE EVERBLADES.

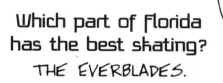

What did the first-time
skater say to Otto?
CAN I CRASH AT YOUR
PLACE TONIGHT?

○○○○ ⇨

THE ROCKETS' BOOKSHELF

Slipped on the Ramp
by Major Y. Pout

Sick Surfing Conditions
by Hy Tide

SURF'S UP!
BY CARA BUNGA

DAREDEVIL
ROCK CLIMBING
BY HUGO FIRST

Stylin' Beachwear
by Sandy Shortz

All About Seals
by C. Lyons

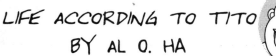

LIFE ACCORDING TO TITO
BY AL O. HA

FIFTY-FOOT WAVES BY GAIL STORM

Bungee Jumping by Adrena Lynn Rush

Reggie Goes Surfing
by C. M. Shredd

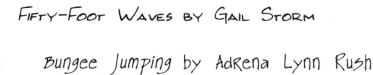

BROKE DAD'S
SURFBOARD
BY I. M. TOAST

0 0 0 0 ⇨

X-TREMELY SCARY SPORTS

How do you feel after a
hockey game with Dracula?
DRAINED.

What do you get when the Invisible
Man rides a Boogie board?
SURFING LIKE YOU'VE NEVER SEEN!

Why do zombies practice extra hard for the skateboard tournament? THE COMPETITION'S REALLY STIFF.

Why didn't the skeleton compete? HE DIDN'T HAVE THE GUTS.

How did Godzilla do? HE CRUSHED THE COMPETITION.

How was the vampire race?
IT WAS NECK AND NECK.

What did the mummy say when Twister finished his film?
"THAT'S A WRAP!"

How do you cheer for a monster?
"YOU GO, GHOUL!"

MAKING WAVES

Why did Otto carry a hammer in his backpack? HE WANTED TO HIT THE BEACH.

What did Otto bring to the school dance?
A BOOGIE BOARD.

Why did Tito join the army?
HE WANTED TO SURF HIS COUNTRY.

What's the difference between a cat and Reggie?
ONE SHEDS, THE OTHER SHREDS!

What did the surfer say to the firefly?
WAY TO GLOW, DUDE!

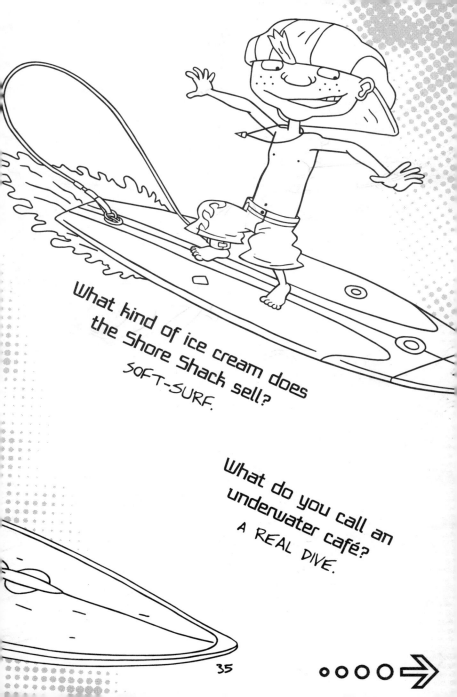

What kind of ice cream does the Shore Shack sell?

SOFT-SURF.

What do you call an underwater café?

A REAL DIVE.

Why did the seashell turn down a date with the starfish?

'CAUSE IT WAS GOING OUT WITH THE TIDE.

What do you do if you surf into a blue whale?

CHEER HIM UP.

What do hippie surfers wear?
ANYTHING TIDE-DYED.

What's Reggie's favorite
ice-cream flavor?
CHOCOLATE-AND-VANILLA TWIST.

○○○○⇨

What do you get
when burglars
go surfing?
A CRIME WAVE.

What do you get when a hairdresser goes surfing?
A PERMANENT WAVE.

What do you get when the sun goes surfing?
A HEAT WAVE.

39

MORE GNARLY KNOCK-KNOCKS

Knock, knock.

Who's there?

Al.

Al who?

Aloha to that, bro!

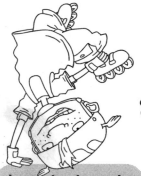

Knock, knock.

Who's there?

Rhoda.

Rhoda who?

Rhoda wave and it was excellent!

Knock, knock.

Who's there?

Board.

Board who?

Board of surfin'— let's go skating!

Knock, knock.

Who's there?

Liz.

Liz who?

Liz go tear up some waves!

Knock, knock.

Who's there?

Gopher.

Gopher who?

Gopher it, dude!

○ ○ ○ ○ ⟹

ROCKET RHYMES

What do you call . . .

An awesome father?

A RAD DAD.

An electrical outlet at Ray's?

A ROCKET SOCKET.

A cooked surfer?
A STEWED DUDE.

A wet winner?
A DAMP CHAMP.

An excellent candle?
A SICK WICK.

A doughnut that plays defensive hockey?
A HOLEY GOALIE.

SIGNS IN OCEAN SHORES

At the Shore Shack:

"IT'S A PLEASURE TO SURF YOU."

46

At the piers on the beach:

"NO SEA-HORSING AROUND."

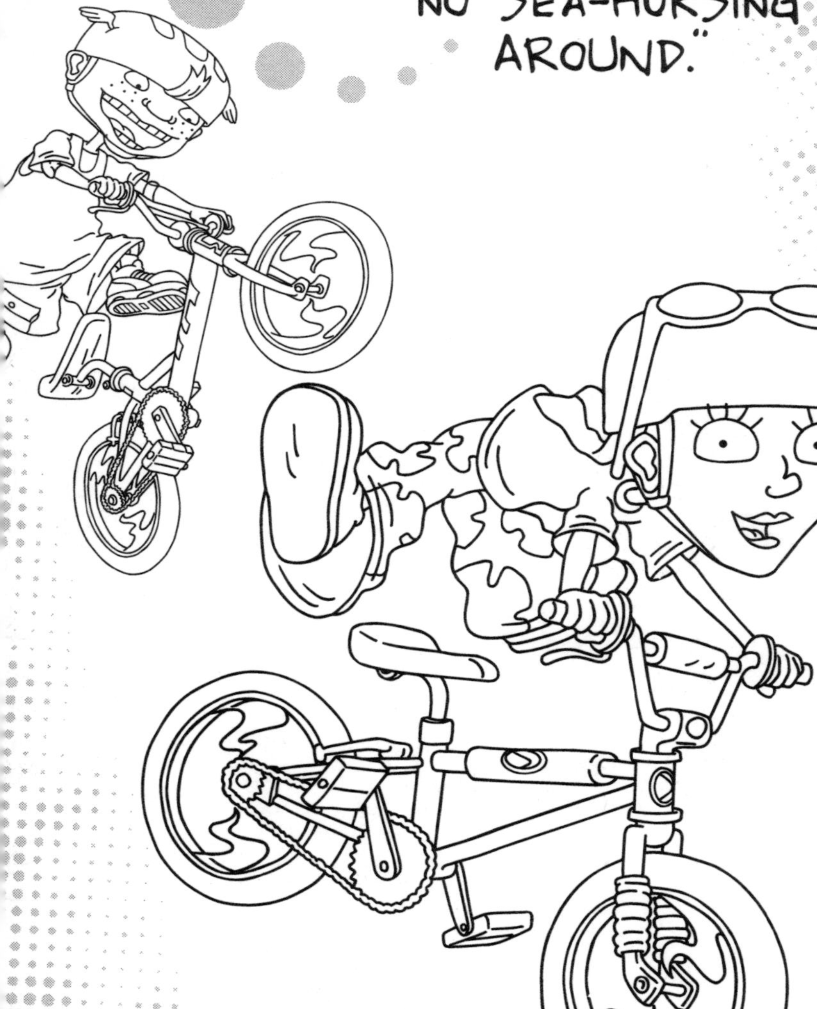